High and Low

A ZEBRA BOOK

Written by David Lloyd
Illustrated by Malcolm Livingstone

PUBLISHED BY

WALKER BOOKS
LONDON

'You always lose your
cuddle,' Polly said to Ben.
Ben's cuddle is a rag.
He won't go to bed without it.

'I'll look high and you
look low,' Polly said.
Ben looked low. No cuddle.
Polly looked high. No cuddle.

'Let's be dogs,' Polly said. 'Dogs can find things with their noses.'

Polly sniffed high.
Ben sniffed low.
No cuddle.

Polly was a horse.
Ben was a rider.
Horse and rider went searching
all over the land.
High and low.
No cuddle.

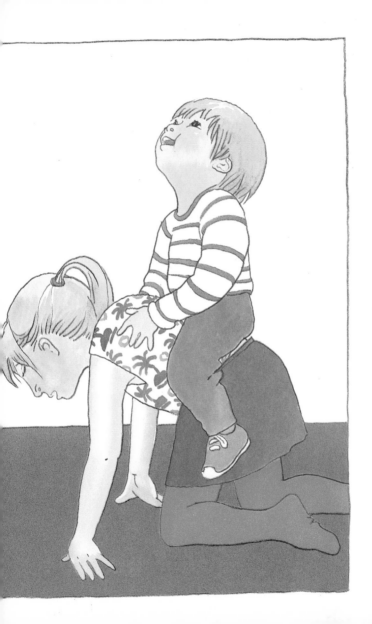

Ben looked very, very low.
Right at the floor.
Polly looked very, very high.
Right at the ceiling.
No cuddle.

Polly made herself small.
'I'm small and you're big,' she said.
'Big people don't need cuddles.'
Ben made a horrible face.
'Cuddle,' he said.

'I'm bored,' Polly said.
'You're always losing your cuddle.'
Ben became a fearful, sliding,
slobbering beast.
The beast said, 'Cuddle.'

Ben and Polly were both beasts.
The beasts moaned and groaned,
searching high and low.
No cuddle.

The beasts began to make a boat.
They could sail across the high seas,
looking for the cuddle.

The boat was ready.
Everyone was aboard.
'I'll be the captain,' Polly said.
'You can be the sailor.
We'll call our boat The Cuddle.'

'High wind, high waves,' Polly said. 'This is the wild, wild sea.' Ben hid low down in the boat. No cuddle.

Low down in the boat
Ben found something.
A hat with something in it.
He put on the hat
and saluted Captain Polly.

Polly took the hat
and saluted Sailor Ben.
The something in the hat
stayed on the sailor's head.
'Cuddle,' said Ben.
'Bedtime,' said Polly.